The Adventures of NICKELODEON JIMMY NEUTRON BOY GENIUS

No More Mr. Smart Guy

by Adam Beechen
based on the teleplay by Jed Spingarn
illustrated by Tom LaPadula

Ready-to-Read

Simon Spotlight/Nickelodeon
New York   London   Toronto   Sydney   Singapore

Based on the TV series *The Adventures of Jimmy Neutron, Boy Genius*®
as seen on Nickelodeon®

SIMON SPOTLIGHT
An imprint of Simon & Schuster Children's Publishing Division
1230 Avenue of the Americas
New York, New York 10020

Manufactured in the United States of America

First Edition

2 4 6 8 10 9 7 5 3 1

Library of Congress Cataloging-in-Publication Data
Beechen, Adam.
No more Mr. Smart Guy / by Adam Beechen.
p. cm. – (Ready-to-read ; #3)
Based on the TV series The adventures of Jimmy Neutron, boy genius.
Summary: Tired of being a boy genius, Jimmy hooks himself up to his Brain-Drain 8000 machine,
but his friends try to reverse the process when they see a meteor headed toward Retroville.
ISBN 0-689-85463-3
[1. Genius–Fiction. 2. Meteors–Fiction. 3. Science fiction.] I. Title. II. Series. PZ7.B383 No 2003
[E]–dc21   2002006302

"Leapin' leptons!"
Jimmy Neutron shouted.
His JuiceBot3000 was supposed to
make fresh-squeezed orange juice.
Instead, his new invention sucked
everything out of the kitchen
and shot it out the window!

The JuiceBot3000 launched
the kitchen appliances all the way
into outer space.
There, the microwave smacked into an
asteroid and became a fiery meteor
headed straight for Retroville!

But the Neutrons did not know
about the meteor. All they knew
was that their kitchen was ruined.
"Look at this mess!" cried Jimmy's
mother. "Sometimes I wish you were
not such a little genius, Jimmy."

At school Jimmy's Magnetic Polarity TV Tray was the best science project in the class . . . again.

And his test scores were the highest in the world . . . again.

"Jimmy, you are so smart, you make us look bad," his classmates complained.

"What is the point of being a genius
if it makes everyone miserable . . .
including me," Jimmy mumbled glumly.
Then he had a brilliant idea.
Who says I have to be smart?
he thought.

Later in his lab, Jimmy showed
Carl and Sheen his latest invention.
"It is the Brain-Drain 8000,"
he told them.
"It will make me normal,
just like everyone else!"

Jimmy put on the helmet
and pulled a lever.
Carl and Sheen watched as
lights flashed and gears whirred.

When the lights stopped flashing,
Carl took the Brain-Drain 8000
off Jimmy's head
and looked closely at his friend.
"Jimmy," he asked, "did it work?"
Jimmy did not answer.

Carl started to get worried.
"Jimmy?" he asked a little louder.
"Did the Brain-Drain 8000 work?"
Jimmy reached out
and grabbed the helmet.
"Oooh, shiny!" he exclaimed.
"I think it worked,"
Sheen said confidently.

Carl and Sheen tested Jimmy.

"Okay," Carl began.

"Tell me what comes next: A, B, C . . ."

"Uhh," Jimmy said, "France?"

"It *did* work!" Sheen exclaimed.

Jimmy's brain was so drained, he listened to his father, Hugh, talk about his decoy collection for two whole hours!

At school Jimmy answered a question wrong for the very first time.

"Class, what is the square root of 144?" Mrs. Fowl asked.

"Eleventy-six!" Jimmy shouted.

Nobody liked the new Jimmy
more than Cindy Vortex.
"I cannot believe it," she said.
"I am smarter than Jimmy Neutron!"

Just then Libby looked
out the window and yelled,
"A meteor . . . and it is headed
for Retroville!"
"We are doomed!" Sheen cried.
"Oooh," Jimmy said, unaware that
his invention had created the
meteor. "Pretty rock thingy."

Minutes later
the mayor of Retroville arrived.
"Neutron, how do we destroy
this meteor?" he asked.
"I like cookies," Jimmy told him.
"To City Hall," the mayor ordered
his assistants. "The boy says
we have cookies to bake!"

21

The kids dragged Jimmy
back to his lab.
"I cannot believe I am about to
say this . . . you are the only one
who can save us," Cindy pleaded.
"How do we make you smart again?"
Jimmy thought hard, but all he
could say was, "Heh, heh,
funny monkey."

The kids dragged Jimmy
back to his lab.
"I cannot believe I am about to
say this . . . you are the only one
who can save us," Cindy pleaded.
"How do we make you smart again?"
Jimmy thought hard, but all he
could say was, "Heh, heh,
funny monkey."

Just then Goddard's video screen popped up.

"Look!" said Cindy, pointing to the video of Jimmy using the Brain-Drain 8000.

"All we have to do is pull the lever on his stupid helmet to make him smart again."

Cindy adjusted the helmet
and put it on Jimmy's head. She
pulled the lever. Lights flashed.
Gears whirred.
When it stopped, she looked Jimmy
in the eye.
"Are you back to your show-off
genius self now?" she asked.

"What is genius but
   an artificial construct in the guise
   of an empirical truth?"
   Jimmy answered.
"We did not understand a word."
   Carl and Sheen cheered. "It worked!"

After learning about the meteor,
Jimmy attached the magnetic plates
from his science project
to his rocket.
"Turbines to speed!" he yelled.
"LIFTOFF!"

Jimmy knew he only had one chance
to stop the meteor.
He checked his calculations
and pushed a red button.
"Eat magnet, space rock!" he shouted.
The magnetic plates sent out
their beam, and the meteor
bounced back into space.
Retroville was saved!

The crowd cheered as Jimmy landed.
"Tell everyone how I helped you,
Neutron," Cindy demanded.
"I am sorry, miss," Jimmy replied.
"Do I know you?"

30

"Playing dumb? Very funny, brain boy.
Next time you almost
destroy the world,
do not come crying to me!"
She stormed away.

"We are glad you are smart again, Jimmy," said Carl.

"Me too," Jimmy agreed. "Hey, did I do anything embarrassing when I was stupid?"

"Oh," Sheen said, "only about eleventy-six times!"